Created by
Jim Jinkins

CHRONICLES

Funnie Family Vacation

by Pam Muñoz Ryan

Illustrated by
William Presing and Tony Curanaj

Funnie Family Vacation is hand-illustrated by the same
Grade A Quality Jumbo artists who bring you
Disney's Doug, the television series.

New York

Disney's

Doug™

Created by
Jim Jinkins

CHRONICLES

Funnie Family
Vacation

CHAPTER ONE

"Okay, Funnie family, load 'em up!" said Phil Funnie as he tied a sleeping bag on top of the car. "We're headed for the Poulet Mountains—fresh air, clean lakes, and the great outdoors!"

"Perfect," Doug groaned. He couldn't believe it. Of all the weeks for a family vacation, his parents had to pick this one.

Porkchop appeared with his television and satellite dish. Judy came out of the house with a CD player, bongo drums, and a week's supply of incense.

"Absolutely not!" said Phil. "This is going to be a *real* camping trip. We're going to experience nature, sleep under the stars, and 'rough it.' Take only what's absolutely necessary."

"Father," said Judy, "isn't it enough that I have to miss the Shakespeare on Ice tryouts this year?"

"Judy, I thought you weren't trying out because you don't know how to skate," said Doug.

Judy glared at him. "Wrong, Dougie. I may not have a great lutz to perform, but I am an *artiste* and I'll be missing something noble and important. What are *you* giving up to go on this family disaster? Huh, Dougie?"

"Stuff," said Doug. He didn't want to tell Judy about missing Beebe's annual swim party. All of his friends would be there, including Patti. There was going to be a live band, and even worse, Guy Graham would be there. All the girls—even Patti—were talking about what a cool upperclassman he was. And Skeeter had told him that Beebe said Guy and Patti would make a cute couple! Now all Doug could think about was Patti and Guy swimming around the pool together. He just knew he'd come home to find out that Patti had fallen for Guy.

"Bring only the bare essentials!" said Dad, snapping Doug out of his daydream.

Porkchop pulled a cooler of Peanutty Buddies closer to the car.

Judy carried an enormous book of plays by Shakespeare.

Doug had already packed his Tendertoe camping gear but he went back inside and got some Man-O-Steelman comic books, his

journal, and his banjo. After all,
Dad had said "the bare
essentials."

"One of you is going to have to
sit in the middle of the backseat
because of Cleopatra Dirtbike's
car seat," said Theda Funnie.

"I already called 'window'," said Judy, sneering at Doug.

Doug groaned again. He'd be smashed between a drooling toddler and Judy, who didn't want to be on a family vacation any more than he did.

How did I get into this mess? he thought.

CHAPTER TWO

"Are we there yet?" asked Doug.

"Nope. First we have to get to Big Bear Mountain. Then we look for the turnoff to Bear Claw Campground," said Phil.

"Is it my imagination or is everything around here named 'Bear Something'?" asked Judy.

"Well, hundreds of years ago bears used to roam all over these

Poulet Mountains," said Phil. "But nobody has seen one in over fifty years."

"It's just not civilized to be spending our vacation in the wilderness with wild animals and . . . and sticks!" said Judy.

"Ju-dee, Judy Funnie, queen of the wild frontier," sang Doug.

"Stop it!" yelled Judy.

"Now, children, we still have a lot of driving to do. Settle down back there," said Theda. "Does anyone want to play a travel game?"

"No way!" said Doug and Judy at the same time.

Judy stared out the window.

Doug leaned his head against the backseat. I'm trapped, he thought. I'm trapped with Judy for a week. I'm going to miss the best party of the summer with a live band and when I get back home, Patti will probably be in love with Guy. He closed his eyes, tilted his head into Dirtbike's car seat, and soon fell asleep.

Doug woke up to an almost empty car and Judy's laughter.

"Where's Mom, Dad, and Dirtbike, and what's so funny?" asked Doug.

"They're diaper-changing. And THIS," said Judy, holding up Doug's journal, "is so funny! It's

positively charming, especially
this part about saving Patti from
Guy, the Uppity Upperclassman!"
  Doug grabbed his journal.
  "You just wait!" said Doug.

"Oh, for heaven's sake, Dougie, stop acting like your life is interesting or important. It was just childish drivel. Get over it."

Doug was angry but there was nothing he could do to get back at Judy, yet, especially since Mom and Dad were coming back to the car with Dirtbike.

Later, when they stopped for lunch, Doug finished eating first and didn't want to spend any more time with Judy than he had to. He decided to wait in the car. That's when he spied Judy's diary in her backpack.

When the family got back to the car Doug and Porkchop were

holding their sides in laughter
and reading Judy's diary.

She screamed, "AHHHH! My
diary!!! My innermost thoughts!
My privacy has been invaded.
Mother and Father, I protest!"

Theda rolled her eyes at Phil.

"Come on, Funnies!" said Phil. "Doug, show a little respect for Judy's privacy. How would you like it if she read *your* journal?"

"But Dad," exclaimed Doug, "she *did*!"

"Oh," said Phil. "Well, both of you were wrong. Now, apologize and let's have some fun. We're on vacation!"

"Sorry," mumbled Doug.

"Sorry," Judy replied.

But as they climbed back into the car, Judy whispered into his ear, "This means war. You better watch your back. I'll get you, Dougie, and your little dog, too!"

"Huh?" said Porkchop.

Doug was furious. His parents were no help. Not only did he have to apologize to Judy even though she had read his journal first, now he had to watch his back to avoid her revenge. Some vacation this was going to be!

CHAPTER THREE

"Finally, Bear Claw Campground!"
said Phil Funnie.

Doug looked at the campsite.
There was an old picnic table, a
fire ring, and a water faucet. That
was all. They were surrounded by
pine trees, and trails that led into
the Poulet wilderness.

Dirtbike bent over, picked up a
bug, and held it up to show them.

"This place is positively primitive!" said Judy.

"Yes, isn't it wonderful?" said Theda.

"Okay, family, everybody help unpack," said Phil.

While they were setting up camp, Doug kept an eye on Judy and set up his pup tent as far away from her as possible.

Before dinner, and right in front of his parents, Judy came over to Doug and held out a bouquet of wildflowers.

"Here, Doug," she said, smirking at him. "It's a peace offering."

"Oh, isn't that nice!" said Theda.

Doug's mind raced. What was Judy up to? Were the flowers full of spiders? Or maybe poison ivy?"

"No thanks! I'm not falling for your tricks, Judy," said Doug. "Get those 'flowers' away from me!"

"Doug, Doug, Doug," said Judy,

shaking her head. "Honestly, it's just an innocent bouquet of wild-flowers. And they say *I'm* the dramatic one in the family!"

"It was a very nice thought," said Phil. "Doug, you could appreciate your sister more."

Judy made a big production of arranging the wildflowers in a jar on the picnic table.

"Stop pretending to be nice!" Doug whispered to Judy.

Judy stuck her tongue out at Doug.

Phil and Theda made a camp-fire and they all roasted hot dogs. Doug was beginning to relax in the warmth of the fire.

"Ketchup, Doug?" asked Judy, smiling a little too sweetly.

Doug panicked. What could she have done to the ketchup? She could have replaced it with hot sauce. That's it. Hot sauce.

"Uh, no thank you," said Doug.

"But you love ketchup," said Theda.

"Not anymore," said Doug.

Doug watched as his mother took the ketchup bottle and put some on her own hot dog.

"Noooo!" cried Doug and he grabbed Theda's hot dog and threw it into the fire.

"Douglas!" said his father. "What on earth are you doing?"

Then Doug noticed ketchup
from the same bottle on his dad's
half-eaten hot dog. There had
been nothing wrong with the
ketchup. It was just Judy playing
mind games again.

He knew he would seem dopier if he tried to explain. "Um, I'm kinda tired. I think I'll turn in early," he said lamely.

Doug left the campfire. He crawled into his sleeping bag and Porkchop crawled into his.

"I'm miserable. I'm missing the best party of the year," said Doug, "and now I have to worry about Judy. And so do you."

"Rouwww," whined Porkchop.

CHAPTER FOUR

The next morning, Judy was gone
when Doug got up. Before lunch,
she hurried into camp wearing a
crown of flowers in her hair.

"Doug, you have to come and
see what I found!"

"Oh, sure, Judy," said Doug. "I'm
going to follow you into the woods
and see what you've found? I
don't think so."

"I know I was mad at you before but I have temporarily forgiven you, dear brother. Anyway, it's something even your simple little brain will appreciate. It's something magnificent! It's right through the woods."

"No thanks," said Doug.

She grabbed Doug's shoulders, looked him in the eyes, and said, "I promise by all that's thespian, you won't be disappointed!"

"Doug, this *is* a family vacation," said Phil. "I think it's time you and Judy did something together. Even if it's just going for a walk."

"But, Dad . . . " protested Doug.

"Your father's right, dear," said Theda. "Why don't you take the baby and Porkchop, too? You can take your lunches with you. Go on now. And be happy."

Doug sighed. At least there was safety in numbers. He and Porkchop followed Judy and Dirtbike into the woods.

Judy kept talking. "Doug, you're never going to believe this. It's the most incredible thing I've ever seen. I was walking along the trail and it just ended at this wall of thick shrubbery and I wondered what was on the other side. . . ."

Doug had to admit that Judy seemed to be excited about something. But what?

They came to the place where the trail ended. There was a wall of bushes, just like Judy said.

"Just push your way through," said Judy.

"Then I fall into a pit or land in a booby trap, right?" said Doug.

"Don't be ridiculous," said Judy.

If Judy was paying him back, he figured he might as well get it over with. He shoved the bushes and tree limbs out of the way. "Keep going," hollered Judy from behind them. "You're almost there, Dougie."

Porkchop whimpered.

Doug could see a clearing on the other side of the bushes. He closed his eyes, took a few steps into the clearing, then opened his eyes.

CHAPTER FIVE

Doug blinked in the sun. At first he couldn't figure out where he was or what he was looking at, but Judy was right. It was incredible.

On the other side of the bushes, Doug found himself standing on what appeared to be a stage. It was overgrown with vines and grass, but it was a stage. And in front of him were row upon row of stone steps, partly covered in grass, that went up the mountainside.

"It's amphitheater ruins," said Judy.

"Ampha . . . what?" asked Doug.

"An outdoor theater," said Judy.

Judy walked across the stage with her arms outstretched. "I can't believe I found it. It must have been here for years and years. Think of the actors who played on this stage. They probably performed *Othello* and *Macbeth* under the stars. You see, Dougie, I needed you to come

along because I need an audience. Now, you and Dirtbike and Porkchop go sit out there."

Doug and Porkchop looked at each other sadly. Instead of fishing or hiking they were going to have to watch Judy put on a play.

Doug ate his lunch while Judy strutted around the stage. His mind wandered to what was going on back at home. Today was the day of Beebe's party. Guy was probably there by now and Patti was probably swooning over him. All of Doug's friends were probably splashing around in the pool, playing games, and listening to the live band.

"Doug!" yelled Judy. "Your turn. Now, I will direct."

"Huh?" said Doug.

"You will perform. Just follow my directions. Now, let's go with that Uppity Upperclassman theme. I liked that, Dougie. Very creative. Here . . . "

She handed him a stick.

"Here's your sword. Now, get into the role. Pretend you are saving a damsel in distress from this uppity guy. Hmmm. That would be Porkchop. Porkchop, be a canine villain," ordered Judy.

Then she picked up Dirtbike. "Come on, sweetie, you are going to be the damsel in the tower."

Doug followed Judy's directions
and he had to admit that he sort
of liked it. Porkchop was a great
bad guy and Doug loved saving

the damsel, even if she did drool on him.

Doug was having so much fun, he didn't even realize how late it

was until Judy said, "Time to take a bow. Imagine thunderous applause."

Judy, Porkchop, Dirtbike, and Doug bowed to the audience as the sun set behind the mountain.

"Judy, it gets dark fast in the mountains," said Doug. "Do you know the way back?"

CHAPTER SIX

"Of course I know the way back," said Judy. "Our campsite is this way."

They followed her into the woods. Doug didn't want to mention that it seemed like they were walking in a circle. Soon they were back at the amphitheater.

Judy pointed in another direction, and said, "Well, maybe it's that way."

"Judy, are we lost?" asked Doug.

Judy looked at him with annoyance. "Of course we're not lost, Dougie! I know exactly where we are! *We* are . . . here. It's our *campsite* that's lost. Why don't you try to help instead of just standing there criticizing me?"

Doug said calmly, "Would my Bluffscout compass and flashlight be useful right now?"

Judy's jaw dropped. She was impressed . . . and relieved. "Way to go, Dougie! That's great! Why don't you lead the way?"

Doug took out his flashlight, got

a bearing with his compass, and
started back to camp.

Doug couldn't resist teasing
Judy. "Ju-dee, Judy Funnie, queen

of the wild frontier," he sang.

"Stop that!" Judy commanded, giving his shoulder a friendly shove.

Doug dropped his flashlight. Before he could pick it up, Judy grabbed his shirt and said, "Dougieeeeeee!"

A huge shadow loomed in front of them.

"Quiet," said Doug.

"No problem. I'm too scared to breathe," whispered Judy.

The shadow looked almost like a bear. It stepped toward them.

"Don't move," said Doug.

"Okay," said Judy. "I can do that. Everyone improvise. Press

yourselves against the rock. Now,
BECOME the rock. BE the rock."

"Judy! Hush!" Doug said des-
perately. Porkchop moaned in
agreement.

"I can't help it," said Judy. "I get this way in life-threatening situations!" she jabbered.

"Jud-eee! Shhh!" Doug said as he watched the bear's shadow lean down, reaching toward them. The shadow's paw was about to touch Judy's head!

Doug couldn't stand it. He turned his head and looked toward the shadow.

He couldn't believe his eyes.

CHAPTER SEVEN

Standing on its hind legs directly in front of the flashlight, and casting a huge shadow on the trail in front of them, was a squirrel. A small squirrel.

It wasn't a bear at all.

"Uh, Judy," said Doug.

"Doug, don't talk. You must experience the rock or you might be the appetizer."

"Judy, look."

Judy turned her head and saw the squirrel. She looked at Dirtbike, Doug, and Porkchop, who were still posed in their rock positions.

She dusted herself off and said calmly, "You were all very good rocks. Now let's get back to camp."

By the time they walked into camp, they were all laughing.

After dinner, around the campfire, they put toasted marshmallows and chocolate pieces on graham crackers. Porkchop invented something new—toasted marshmallows on a Peanutty Buddy cone.

They sat around telling about
the day and the outdoor theater
and especially the "bear."

Doug brought out his banjo and
they sang songs.

This isn't so bad, thought Doug. The whole family is here around the campfire. Dad has his arm around Mom. Dirtbike is chasing a beetle. And Judy seems to have forgotten about me reading her diary. Doug realized that he was actually having fun.

When the fire died down, they all headed for their tents.

"I'm tired," said Doug as he crawled into his sleeping bag.

Porkchop nodded, as he crawled into his.

Doug closed his eyes until Porkchop started whining.

"What is it, boy?" asked Doug as he sat up. And then he saw it.

A bear—a real bear—stared at them through the flap of the tent.

"AHHHHHHHHH!" screamed Doug and Porkchop.

Then they heard Judy laughing.

"Jud-ee, Judy Funnie, queen of the wild frontier!" she sang as she came inside the tent holding a giant bear mask.

"Hey, little brother, it's just a souvenir I picked up at the trading post. Pretty authentic, huh? Thought you'd like it to remember our adventure in the woods."

When Doug and Porkchop untangled themselves from each other, Doug said, "Gee, thanks

Judy. It's . . . it is sorta real-look-
ing and um . . . interesting."

"Think nothing of it. It's just

another of my many sisterly acts of kindness," said Judy. "Good night."

"Good night," said Doug.

CHAPTER EIGHT

By the end of the week, everyone agreed it had been a fun vacation but that they were glad to get home. Porkchop went straight to his tepee and adjusted his satellite dish. Judy called everyone in her drama club to tell them about the amphitheater. Doug headed straight to Mr. Swirly's to see his friends.

"Doug!" said Skeeter. "How was your vacation?"

"You know, Skeet, it really turned out to be more fun than I thought. Fishing and hiking with Dad wasn't as bad as I thought it would be, and even Judy's kinda fun when she's not being weird," said Doug. "How was Beebe's party?"

"Oh, it was the usual," said Skeeter.

"Was everyone there?" asked Doug. He was dying to know about Guy and Patti.

"Yep," said Skeeter. "Everybody was there."

"Well, um, Guy, too?" said Doug.

"He came, Doug. He was pretty doofy, though. He spent the whole time trying to keep his hair dry and in place. Imagine that? At a swim party!"

"Yeah," said Doug. "Imagine that. How was the band?"

"It was okay, if you like marching bands," said Skeeter. "Mr. Fort sure is loud."

Doug realized that all of his worrying had been for nothing.

Beebe, Patti, and Connie walked into Swirly's.

"Hey Doug!" said Patti. "I missed you at Beebe's party."

"You did?" said Doug.

"Sure," said Patti.

Doug smiled. Not going to Beebe's party hadn't been so bad after all. It was funny how things worked out.

That night at dinner, Phil was already talking about next year's vacation.

"How about the Big City? Museums, boat tours, and deli-catessens. What do you say, Funnie family?"

"I couldn't possibly," said Judy. "I've already told everyone in my drama club that we're going back to *my* mountain retreat. They're all coming, too. To perform in the amphitheater and to commune with nature."

"I liked the mountains," said Doug. "And Dirtbike really liked the beetles."

"Father," Judy continued, "the Big City? How ludicrous. It's so removed from nature and inspiration and . . . and sticks."

"Dirtbike's a little young for museums," said Theda.

That's right, thought Doug. Besides, he still had a little unfinished business to take care of. He

still had to get back at Judy for
scaring him with that bear mask.

"Well then, Funnies," said Phil.
"Next year, back to the Poulet
Mountains!"